WHAT I DON'T KNOW MIGHT HURT ME

THINK YOU CAN HANDLE
JAMIE KELLY'S FIRST YEAR OF DIARIES?

AND DON'T MISS . . .

Jim Benton's Tales from Mackerel Middle School

DEAR DUMB DIARY,

YEAR TWO

WHAT I DON'T KNOW MIGHT HURT ME

BY JAMIE KELLY

SCHOLASTIC INC.

No part of this publication may be reproduced, stored in a retrieval system,
or transmitted in any form or by any means, electronic, mechanical,
photocopying, recording, or otherwise, without written permission of the
publisher. For information regarding permission, write to Scholastic Inc.,
Attention: Permissions Department, 557 Broadway, New York, NY 10012.

ISBN 978-0-545-37765-2

Copyright © 2013 by Jim Benton

All rights reserved. Published by Scholastic Inc.
SCHOLASTIC and associated logos are trademarks
and/or registered trademarks of Scholastic Inc.
DEAR DUMB DIARY is a registered trademark of Jim Benton.

12 11 10 9 8 7 6 5 4 3 2   13 14 15 16 17 18/0
Printed in the U.S.A.   40
First printing, July 2013

For the Dicky Flartsnutt in all of us.

Bully for you, Kristen LeClerc, Shannon Penney, Abby McAden, Anna Bloom, Jackie Hornberger, and Yaffa Jaskoll.

THIS DIARY IS THE PROPERTY OF:

Jamie Kelly

SCHOOL: Mackerel Middle School

WHO I CAN COUNT ON: Isabella,

Mom, Dad, Stinker, Stinkette,

ANGELINE

AWESOME SUPERPOWER:

CUPCAKERY

You think that you can just **BULLY** your way into my Diary and start Reading anything you want?

Well,

YOU BIG JERK,

WE HAVE WAYS OF DEALING WITH

BULLIES

even though I'm not exactly sure what they are

Dear Whoever Is Reading My Dumb Diary,

I know you think it's okay to read my diary, and I know that you think that there is **know** way I'll never find out.

But I know I will find out, and when I do, I know you're going to regret it, because I know things like that. You know?

You never know when I'll find out, or where you'll be when I do, but there is **know** escaping it — and you know it.

Knowingly,

Jamie Kelly

Dear Dumb Diary,

Today was the best day ever.
Said nobody.
My mom dropped me off at Isabella's house,
because it's Sunday and that's our main day to do
the homework that was due on Thursday, except
that we got an extra day to turn it in and then
another extra day after that because Isabella told
our teacher that her house had been robbed and the
burglars had stolen our homework. **Again.**

I think the teacher bought it because Isabella
had a sketch of the burglar, which looked really
official because she had me do a drawing of
Abraham Lincoln with long hair. Isabella thinks he
may have been a burglar before he went into
presidenting. (She thinks a full beard without
an accompanying mustache is suspicious.)

We often do our Thursday/Sunday homework
at my house, but since my mom was working on
getting dinner ready, I was concerned that there
was a chance she might try to make us eat it, so I
did what I could to avoid being there. Isabella's

mom, on the other hand, is such a good cook that she could even work at a Burger King or someplace awesome like that.

Unfortunately, Isabella's mean older brothers exist **and** were home, which meant that everybody was on **Extreme Red Alert**. Isabella and her brothers were listening carefully for anything that anybody said to be either:

1) Insulting.
2) Very Insulting.

And, if one of them did say something insulting, the other would say something back that was either:

1) Very Insulting.
2) Astonishingly Insulting.
3) Insulting enough that it could get repeated to a psychologist twenty years from now.

Then it was the first person's turn again. It was a lot like people playing tennis, but instead of a tennis ball, they used a dirty diaper full of **wasps and grenades**.

One of these fights broke out (because one always does), and it became so intense that at one point they were exchanging insults about each other's mothers.

"Your mother is so ugly that the mirrors charge extra to reflect her," Isabella spat.

"Oh, yeah, well, your mother is so fat, she has different weather on her front than she does on her back," one of her brothers said.

Here's the thing: Isabella and her brothers have the **same** mother, and she walked in just as they were exchanging these insults.

"So this is what my kids think of me?" she asked angrily.

"No, Mom," Isabella said, and ran up to her and gave her a big hug.

"So you think I'm fat?" her mom said quietly, the way the hissing fuse on a stick of **dynamite** is pretty quiet.

"No, no. Don't you remember? I was the one that said you were ugly."

By the time my mom got there, Isabella's mom had screamed until her voice was hoarse, and I had to go home early and eat the dinner my mom had made (a big salad, which she had somehow **badly burned**). Plus, I had to finish my homework by myself, which is one of the nine worst ways to do homework.

THE NINE WORST WAYS TO DO HOMEWORK

1.	Alone.	6.	While trampled.
2.	On fire.	7.	Without music.
3.	Thoroughly.	8.	Immersed in fart.
4.	While buried.	9.	In hieroglyphics.
5.	Toothlessly.	10.	There are only 9.

MONDAY 02

Dear Dumb Diary,

You might recall, Dumb Diary, that Isabella and I joined some clubs last month, since my Uncle Dan (who is also the assistant principal at my school) kind of demanded it.

It's hard to know what to call your uncle when he is also the assistant principal. Away from school, I go with Uncle Dan. At school, I go with Mr. Devon or Assistant Principal Devon. In outer space, I go with Devon the OverSeer.*

He didn't actually **demand** that I join clubs. He did that thing where an adult says that they think something would be a *good idea*, but deep down you know that's kind of like when a pirate tells you that they think swimming would be a *good idea* after they make you walk the plank. Nobody is really **demanding** that you swim. You make up your own mind. "Swim," they say, "if you think that's what's best."

*Haven't actually had the chance to use this one yet.

But the problem with clubs is that they expect you to participate. Isabella also thinks it's deceptive that they don't give us **actual clubs**, but that's another story.

I joined the Cuisine Club, which is taught by my gorgeous art teacher, Miss Anderson. We learn how to prepare wonderfully delicious dishes that are so beautiful to behold that it seems wrong to eat them, in the same way that people don't feel they should eat beautiful paintings.

Isabella joined the Videogamer Club, not really because she's that into video games, but because she knows how much it will irritate her mean older brothers when she gets good enough to beat them, and she likes being **the most beautiful girl** in the entire club.

Okay, the only beautiful girl.

Okay, the only girl.

Okay, a girl*ish* person in the club.

"*Beauty is in the eye of the beholder and also in his mouth.*"

THIS SHOULD BE OUR MOTTO.

Isabella and I are also co-presidents of the Student Awareness Committee, which is a club we invented in order to get credit for joining a club. Originally, just I was the president, but Isabella and I felt that both of us should be president, and I wanted her to get up off my stomach.

It sounds pretty official, and you would assume that any club we started would be a **Bustin'-Out-the-Drawers-Party-Spaceship-O-Fun**, but frankly, we're already kind of bored with it. We just sit there and discuss what we're aware of, and as it turns out, we're just not aware of many things.

As the presidents, Isabella and I decided the club should meet on Wednesdays, which is when she and I attend other clubs so that we can never attend the Student Awareness Committee meetings. This makes Angeline, the secretary, angry, but we told her that if she's ever aware of something she can email us and we'll consider becoming aware of it, too. Problem solved.

Isabella and I
co-deciding she
should be a
co-president

We've discovered that this is the time of year when all of the clubs have their **"membership drives,"** where they try to recruit more members. The school actually gives a prize to the club that increases their numbers by the highest percentage.

They do this because:

1) The school just does things like this.
2) There is no other reason.
3) Why are you still reading the list? I told you back at number 2 that there were no other reasons.

I can't imagine this being a very big deal, anyway.

SCHOOLS OFTEN DO THINGS FOR NO GOOD REASON

THEY TEACH EARLY IN THE MORNING WHEN YOU'RE TIRED AND QUITE STUPID.

THEY SERVE LUNCH AT NOON WHEN YOU'RE TIRED AND NOT HUNGRY.

THEY TEACH IN THE AFTERNOON WHEN YOU'RE TIRED AND QUITE STUPID.

TUESDAY 03

Dear Dumb Diary,

So now Angeline has to go and be aware of something. Just when I was pretty sure we could let the Student Awareness Committee quietly die a **dignified death**, like some majestic old elephant or the Square Dancing Club, Angeline has to be aware of something. Great.

And, of course, it couldn't be something interesting like nail polish or why maybe there should be a special class in nail polish and how to get it out of your beagle's ear. (Mom, if you're reading this, I'm not admitting anything. Somebody else could have painted a heart in his ear.)

Angeline just had to be aware of one of those **THINGS THAT ADULTS LIKE.**

Stinker was also probably the one who spilled the NAIL POLISH IN THE KITCHEN WHILE HE DID IT!

SORRY, STINKS. YOU'RE SO BUSTED.

She stopped us right in front of the office where Assistant Principal Devon happened to be standing. Oh, yeah, right. Like **that** wasn't totally planned. She probably laid out some sort of bait that attracts assistant principals, like neckties dipped in coffee.

"Mr. Devon," Angeline squeaked, "I was wondering if the Student Awareness Committee could count on you for your support for some work we want to do regarding bullying."

Isabella stepped forward.

"Who do you need bullied, Angeline? I **got this**."

Uncle Dan looked at Isabella as if she had just volunteered to **burp on his breakfast**.

Then he said we could count on his full support, since the school faculty is always looking for ways to reduce bullying.

Angeline nodded at me with this big smile, like I was going to nod and smile back the way that dorks do in dorky TV shows about dorks doing dorky stuff at school.

Sorry, Blondie, I don't do dork. The best I could do was hiss a weak sound of false approval through the thin sliver of a fake smile.

I didn't want to be all **negative** or anything.

I'm always positive even when I would rather lick fungus off a dead rat's eyeball that I dragged out of a garbage disposal in an abandoned insane asylum because I am sweet and I am classy.

Dear Dumb Diary,

So today after school, I went to the Cuisine Club, which, I may have mentioned, is taught by Miss Anderson, who is extraordinarily lovely and therefore shares with me that special bond that **truly beautiful people** have.

You know how it is, Dumb Diary. You'll see a couple of us standing around looking amazing, laughing attractively about something pretty, and you'll think, "**Gosh**. Why can't the whole world be that glamorous?" But you would never say it out loud, because if you did, we'd just look at you from behind our three-inch-long eyelashes and smirk glamorously, and you would wither and crumble right there on the spot and we'd giggle prettily at your steaming remains.

In your case, Dumb Diary, we'd also probably discuss how **weird** it was that a diary talked.

The steaming remains of the unattractive

are also fairl unattractive.

Miss Anderson was focusing on salads today, because with all the colors and textures, they're sort of like bouquets you can eat. You know, if you poured dressing all over your bouquets.

Isabella doesn't really like vegetables. She says that vegetables aren't food — vegetables are what food **eats**. It's probably best that she didn't join this club.

At the end of the class, Miss Anderson told us that we have to try to get more people to sign up for our club, because she really wants to win this membership competition. There are nine kids in the Cuisine Club right now, and only so many kids left in the school with their Wednesday afternoons free.

She gave us a goal: By next week, we're all supposed to have signed up three other kids.

Should be a **breeze**.

You never want to admit bad things about the people you love, like your grandma, or your dad, or **yourself**. I can imagine Dracula's granddaughter at his trial, being all like, "Yeah, well, lots of people probably have blood that is way too delicious and it's their own fault."

So I hate to admit that my grandma is not a Dracula, but she is a *Gitoffma*. That's one of those old people who shouts at kids who walk or ride bikes across their lawns.

Other Oldsters

The SUZYMARYFRED
Can never get your name right

SUZY
MARY
FRED
BILBO

THE **WHERESMA**
Always misplaces stuff

where's ma glasses? where's ma Glasses?

THE **GRAMMARMA** AND **GRAMMARPA**
Always corrects you

NO... say: "Isabella and **I** are going to kidnap a koala."

"Gitoffmalawn!" they yell, and then stab their canes in the air threateningly as if they are trying to shish kebab any invisible children that have wandered too close.

Gitoffmas are under the impression that, while grass can endure mountains of snow, blistering sun, thunderstorms, and driving winds, if a forty-five-pound child steps on it, it will instantly die. It is as if nature has struck this delicate balance so that old people **freak out** about their lawns, and in turn, the lawns give them something to **freak out** about.

I found out today that my grandma, in her haste to give a child nightmares, rushed out onto her porch to yell at one, took a few hilarious steps into the sky, fell back to Earth, and broke her hip, which is what old people break most (after wind).

Dad said that this means that Mom has to go stay with Grandma for a while to help her get around, and maybe yell at kids if the pain medications Grandma is on keep her from swearing well.

I asked why Aunt Carol couldn't go, and it's because Aunt Carol went and stayed with Grandma a couple years ago when she broke her **other** hip when she ran off the porch to yell at a moth that appeared to be preparing to land on her lawn.

So it's going to just be me and Dad at home for a while. I'm sure it won't be a big deal.

GRANDMA'S MEDICAL HISTORY

SPRAINED MOUTH BELLOWING AT REALITY SHOW

INJURED TONGUE BY OVERSUCKING A BUTTERSCOTCH

DISLOCATED SHOULDER TRYING ON BATHING SUIT THAT WAS SIX SIZES TOO SMALL

DISLOCATED OTHER SHOULDER REMOVING THAT BATHING SUIT

BROKE FINGER BY OVER-WAGGING DURING FURIOUS LECTURE

INJURED KNEE TRYING TO PUSH OPEN DOOR LABELED "PULL"

BUNIONS BECAUSE OLD PEOPLE SEEM TO LIKE GETTING THESE.

WHAT THE HECK ARE THEY ANYWAY?

THURSDAY 05

Dear Dumb Diary,

At lunch today, Angeline presented some of her ideas for the Student Awareness Committee's Anti-Bullying Campaign.

"Bullying is a huge problem," Angeline said.

"Why's that?" Isabella asked, taking a bite from a sandwich she had recently acquired from a much smaller classmate.

"How would you like it if you were bullied?" Angeline asked.

Isabella snorted and I snorted along with her. We **co-snorted**.

I have to believe that getting a CO-SNORT from us is pretty devastating.

"Isabella's mean older brothers are the biggest bullies in the world," I said. "Isabella knows more about being bullied than anybody."

Angeline's big pretty blue eyes got bigger and prettier and bluer, which was **revolting**.

"You're perfect for this!" she said in a voice so high that I stuck my fingers in my ears. Somewhere, a dog piddled.

"Tell me, Isabella," Angeline said breathlessly, "what would you say that people need to do in order to stop being bullied?"

"So far, Angeline, nothing I've tried has worked," Isabella said, chewing her sandwich slowly.

Angeline's face fell like a bag of hammers with a **really nice** complexion.

HEY.
PEOPLE.
When you are DISTRESSED ABOUT Something...

you really have a RESPONSIBILITY to look a LITTLE GROSS. PEOPLE.

Isabella stood up and walked away.

"I knew her brothers were bad," Angeline said. "But I had **no** idea. **Poor Isabella.**"

I quickly clamped my hand over Angeline's mouth.

"Don't ever say '*poor Isabella*' again. Seriously, Angeline, you will be dead before you hit the ground if she hears anything like pity coming out your mouth. Her brothers are monsters, but she doesn't want anybody's help."

Angeline nodded, and I removed my hand and looked at the film of lip gloss that remained there.

It was a little gross, but I have to give her mad props on the lip-gloss selection. My palm had never looked more kissable.

I'm pretty sure I saw my foot flirting with it.

When I got home, Dad was there with some plans for while Mom's gone. He doesn't know how to work the dishwasher, washing machine, or food. He has never cleaned anything, and I don't think he knows how.

But he believes he has a way to not do **anything** sloppy around the house until Mom gets back.

Mom can't stand coming home to a messy house, and neither one of us want to take that heat.

DAD HAS SOME IDEAS

HOP AROUND ON ONE FOOT AND CUT SOCK LAUNDERING IN HALF!

Prepare meals INSIDE GARBAGE BAGS! No dishes to wash and CLEANUP IS A Breeze!

Just Live in car until Mom comes home.

FRIDAY 06

Dear Dumb Diary,

This morning, Dad served breakfast standing up on the front porch so that we wouldn't get any crumbs on the floor.

We ate Pop-Tarts, but I was only allowed to peel back a small section of the wrapper and nibble tiny sections at a time because he didn't want to sweep the front porch, either.

And amazingly, this wasn't the most disturbing **pastry-related event** of the day.

When I got to school, Angeline was in the front lobby, handing out free cupcakes and trying to recruit people to sign up for the Student Awareness Committee.

Yeah, that's right: Signing up the people who should be rightfully signing up for the Cuisine Club.

Look, I hate getting all presidenty, but it was the only thing I could do. Besides, I actually **do** like it a little bit.

"Hey," I said presidentially. "Pretty sure you need the **CLUB PRESIDENT'S** authorization to do something like this." And I said it in all capital letters, just like that.

"I have it," she said, and gestured toward a chimpanzee huddled in the corner eating a pile of cupcakes.

CHOMP
GOBBLE
SNORT
GLUT
SLOBBER

Okay. Not a **REAL** chimpanzee, but Isabella can resemble one when she is hunched over and eating. A **girlpanzee**.

I walked right over and started to complain, but Isabella knew what I was going to say.

"Tell that story walking," she said. "My brothers ate everything in the house and I didn't have anything to eat this morning. I'd authorize Angeline to have a **Unicorn Roast** if it meant I got cupcakes for breakfast."

"You realize that this means she's going to snap up all the kids who have their Wednesdays free, right?" I asked.

"I wouldn't worry about that," Isabella said through a thick clot of frosting.

"And why's that?"

"Because worrying about things isn't something I would do when I have a whole pile of cupcakes," she said.

The Girlpanzee in its NATURAL ENVIRONMENT

There's a famous saying that goes, "Fight fire with fire," but now that I think about it, you could also use it to fight hamsters, or tons of other things.

What the saying is *supposed* to mean is that you should use the same type of techniques and strategies your opponent is using. In **this** case, my opponent is Angeline and the fire is cupcakes — delicious, delicious fire.

What Angeline is about to learn is that cupcakes are like little blank pieces of paper to the artistic members of the cooking world, and she is no match for the **full concentrated power of the Cuisine Club**.

While I was writing that I screamed it so loud, my dad burst into my room to see what was going on and startled Stinker, who bit him. Sorry, Dad.

An ARTIST'S Approach to the CUPCAKE

I explained Angeline's unwelcome **Cupcakery** to Miss Anderson. Like me, and all the other attractive people of the world, Miss Anderson is very competitive. She convened a special emergency meeting of the Cuisine Club for a few minutes after school, where she gave the instructions that we are all supposed to bake cupcakes for a free giveaway Monday morning.

I wish I could ask Isabella to help, but since we're both going after the same Wednesday crowd, I think it's best that she doesn't know.

The best thing to do is to keep it a **secret**.

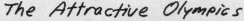

SATURDAY 07

Dear Dumb Diary,

I explained to Dad what I was doing, and he offered to take me to the store and buy cupcakes just so I wouldn't get anything dirty. I explained that the store cupcakes aren't good enough. I'm representing the Cuisine Club here, so that means I **have** to make them.

After his initial panic faded, Dad finally said okay, if I promised that everything would be perfectly clean when I finished. And then he said **"PERFECTLY"** many many many many many many times.

I told him that I would get everything loaded in the dishwasher, cleaned, and put back long before Mom got home.

He was surprised to hear about this object called a "dishwasher."

"What does it do?" he asked.

I got started right away on the cupcakes, and just as I had everything going, I heard the front door open.

"Yes, c'mon in," I heard my dad say. "You can help her bake cupcakes to give away on Monday in order to boost the membership of her club."

Honestly, it was the longest sentence he has ever spoken to Isabella, and the only time I have ever told him what I was doing and he got it straight.

I think Isabella picked up on that, too, and she sauntered in with a smile.

what does Isabella's saunter remind me of? I just can't put my finger on it...

"Cupcakes, huh?" she said accusingly. "What have I told you about baking?"

I didn't want to repeat it, but she slowly lowered a bowl of batter toward Stinker and Stinkette, who snapped at it like a pair of small, obese sharks. She was going to give it to them if I didn't comply.

I recited the rule.

"'If I ever bake anything, or know of something being baked, I am to call you **immediately**. If that's not possible, I am to grab the baked goods and run to your house and make sure I'm not followed.' Please don't let Stinker eat that."

She put the bowl back up on the counter, and Stinker bit a chair leg. He was angry, but he's too smart to bite Isabella after the unpleasantness that we now simply refer to as **Field Goal Stinker**.

BEAGLE SHARKS!

FOAM
SLOBBER
SNAP

SNAP
DROOL

Isabella agreed to help me bake and clean up if she was allowed to eat as many cupcakes as she wanted. Since I knew that would only be three cupcakes at the most, I was fine with that.

Eleven cupcakes later, I realized that the reason I had the number three in my head was probably because that's how many she can fit in her mouth **AT ONE TIME**.

I dropped five others on the floor and the dogs ate four of those and Dad ate one, but that still gives me twenty that I will complete decorating tomorrow.

Isabella cleaned up while I wrangled Stinker and his dogdaughter, Stinkette, out of the house. They both have well-known cupcake issues and would probably devise some kind of attack on the cupcakes if we were both distracted cleaning.

The technique is simple. You just put little chunks of potato into a couple of those cupcake papers, smear some vanilla frosting on them, and throw them outside. The dogs will bolt out the door after them. I call them **cupfakes**.

Next time, I'll let Dad know what I'm doing, because a few minutes later, I saw him out in the yard trying to wrestle the cupfakes away from the dogs.

CUPFAKE
POTATO CHUNK IN
CUPCAKE WRAPPER

SHAMBURGER
PATTY IS MASHED-UP BUN
STAINED WITH SOY SAUCE

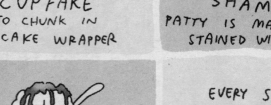

NOWAE SUNDAE
CHOCOLATE SAUCE DRIZZLED
OVER MASHED POTATOES.

EVERY SINGLE ONE
OF THESE IS BETTER
THAN ANYTHING MOM
HAS EVER MADE.

Dear Dumb Diary,

I had a long day ahead of me putting the final touches on the cupcakes, and doing it all by myself was a really good idea . . .

. . . said the pretend girl about something that never happened.

Isabella was over **REALLY EARLY**, because I'm sure that she suspected that there could be gummy worms or M&M's involved in the final stages of cupcake decoration. Let's face it, the **Girl Knows Me.**

I had **20** perfect cupcakes to decorate flawlessly, which meant that I had **19** perfect cupcakes after Isabella got one down before I could stop her.

Actually, **18**, after Dad (seeing Isabella eating one) totally forgot why I was making them in the first place and thought they were up for grabs.

And then Isabella ate another, thinking that Dad eating one signified that I had lost control of the cupcakes and she could get away with it.

17 cupcakes.

Actually, **16**, after Stinker managed to get up on the counter and get one.

I managed to decorate **16** cupcakes. They were so flawlessly regal with gummy worms, M&M's, and an extra layer of frosting that I kept thinking that the reporters from *Cupcake Monthly Magazine* might pull up any moment to photograph them for the cover.

That's silly. I know that there's no such magazine as *Cupcake Monthly*.

But maybe there's a *Gummy Worm Monthly*, and they would be interested.

Isabella doesn't care at all how food looks. She got so bored watching me prepare things that she couldn't eat, she eventually just went and watched TV with my dad. She doesn't really like watching sports much, but she does like violence, and sports have **just enough** to hold her interest. Not that she hasn't shared ideas about how to make sports better.

At one point I felt a little bad for Isabella's dad, who was probably at home at that very instant, wishing that she were there watching TV with him.

But those brothers are hard to deal with.

ISABELLA'S SPORT IMPROVEMENTS

FOOTBALL PLAYED WITH FRESH PIG SKIN

BASEBALL PLAYERS ALLOWED TO CARRY BAT TO BASES

HOCKEY RINK NOT NECESSARILY FROZEN

Isabella stayed for dinner and we ordered a pizza. Dad took out scissors and cut the lid of the pizza box into crude cardboard circles for us to use as plates so we didn't get anything dirty. He also cut out some cardboard forks, and even a cardboard centerpiece.

After dinner, he used Stinker like a **living vacuum cleaner** and dragged him around to eat any little crumbs that might have fallen on the floor, and he also ate a paper napkin, but he's done that before. At some point tomorrow it will start to pass through, and he'll look like a Hershey's Kiss.

Stinker, I mean.

NEVER HAPPIER

MONDAY 09

Dear Dumb Diary,

Dad gave me a ride to school with my ~~16~~ 15 cupcakes. (He wanted one for giving me a ride.)

I set them up on a table in the front lobby with a few other members of the Cuisine Club. Miss Anderson was there, too, wearing an adorable little chef outfit like one you might see when you go shopping for Halloween costumes in the part of the store Mom guides you away from.

My fellow Cuisine Clubbers had also done their best to provide beautiful cupcakes, but let's be honest here, there are **Baked Goods** and there are **Baked Not-So-Goods**.

Angeline had also set up a little table, but there was nothing on hers — nice work, bonehead — and Isabella dragged a table into the lobby just as we finished assembling our glorious offerings.

Baked Goods

Baked Not-So-Goods

FLY WING

Baked Bads

The kids started rolling in, and I was suddenly aware of the fact that lots of these kids wouldn't be joining our club. They were just there to slobber up some free eats.

When Miss Anderson noticed that I was politely jabbing some of them away from the table, she rushed over, as much as somebody *can* rush in adorable chef high heels.

"You can't decide who can have them, Jamie," she whisperyelled. "I know some of these kids won't sign up for the club. That's just how it goes."

And she clicky-clacked back over to her position, where she handed out information on the club and tried to avoid making eye contact with that one custodian who was staring at her like he was really, really into cooking.

Join THE Cuisine Club!

It was all a big success. There were lots of kids standing around the table, gobbling down the jumbo cupcakes with the extra layers of frosting. I was going through the crowds with my clipboard, getting a kid here and there to join the Cuisine Club, when I suddenly noticed that the crowd was starting to migrate over to Angeline's table.

That phrase came back to me: *Fight fire with fire.*

And I realized: You don't fight fire with fire. You fight fire with *water.*

Angeline had pitchers of ice-cold water and little cups that, it turns out, you want DESPERATELY when you are gobbling jumbo cupcakes with an extra layer of frosting.

As the kids were washing down my elaborate cupcakes with her **FREE TAP WATER**, Angeline kept yapping about the Student Awareness Committee.

MY KIDS. MY WEDNESDAY KIDS. ONCE THEY ATE THE CUPCAKES, WHICH WERE MY PERSONAL PROPERTY, THESE KIDS BECAME MY PERSONAL PROPERTY.

GULP
GLURG

SWILL
GULP

I stared complaining to Miss Anderson, but before she could do anything about it, the crowd was migrating again, this time over to Isabella's table. Isabella had set up a TV and a video game that I guess won't even be released for another month. The crowd was into it.

"I guess your brothers don't know you have that game?" I asked.

"Nope."

"You're never going to get girls to sign up this way," I said. "Girls don't like video games."

"Some do," she said. "And besides, do the math. If I get all the boys, and you and Angeline split up the girls, **I WIN**. That's why I suggested she show up here this morning with the water."

I didn't like it, but technically she was right, and there really isn't any other kind of right.

But fortunately, before Isabella and Angeline could complete their evil plans, the first bell rang and everybody had to scramble for class.

This isn't over yet.

When you're right, you're right.

Just do it somplace else, dude.

TUESDAY 10

Dear Dumb Diary,

At lunch today, Angeline asked me to make some anti-bullying posters for the Student Awareness Committee.

"I know that you don't really want to, but you still are one of the presidents of the club and you're probably the best postermaker in the school."

She was wrong about that. There's no *probably* about it.

"FINE," I sighed in such a way that should have made her withdraw the request, but evidently she doesn't know sigh language. "What should they say?"

SIGH LANGUAGE

"I was hoping that you and Isabella could help with that," Angeline said. "There are a lot of things kids get bullied for. Maybe something about physical appearances?"

"I got this," Isabella said. "How about DON'T BE REALLY FAT OR WE'LL BULLY YOU."

A full minute passed where we just stared at Isabella.

"Isabella," Angeline began quietly, as if she were going to attempt to teach algebra to a slow infant, "people can be overweight for many reasons. It can be hereditary, or glandular, or their metabolism —"

Isabella *pffffted* at Angeline.

"Angeline, I don't have time to consult a doctor for a diagnosis every time I see some tub-of-guts walking down the street. I look, maybe I imagine them falling down, I laugh, and then I move on."

Angeline looked shocked and was about to scold Isabella in a way that would not have worked out well for Angeline's nose.

"Angeline, if Isabella never says anything to that person, it's not bullying, is it?" I asked.

"The laughter might be considered bullyish."

"What if the person never heard it?"

"It's still really mean."

Isabella put down her fork and leaned in close to Angeline.

"What if I notice that somebody has really dorky shoes, and I tell them so, and they do something about it, and eventually they're much happier because I told them? **You** wouldn't tell them, Angeline. Jamie probably wouldn't, either. So who's the bad guy now? I helped, and **you didn't**."

Angeline wasn't sure how to answer that one, and neither was I.

Isabella was **right**.

Isabella can really get in your face

"Hang on," Angeline said. "What about if that person couldn't afford any other shoes, or had to wear them for some reason you didn't know about?" She smiled her smug little smile right in Isabella's face. "Then **you** would be the bad guy, Isabella. **YOU** would."

Isabella laughed.

"You got me there, Ang, but you may have overlooked one little thing."

"Oh, really? What's that?"

"Some of us don't really **care** if we're the bad guy."

Angeline looked as if she had been punched in her perfect gut. She glanced at me for some kind of support, but I had none to give. Isabella is who she is.

"Let's talk about the posters tomorrow," I said. I just didn't have the energy to explain to the perky blond that the real world isn't all magical like *The Wizard of Oz*, and even if it was, Isabella would be the monkey with the most frequent-flyer miles of all.

Hey! Take it easy! I don't want the shoes that bad!

WEDNESDAY 11

Dear Dumb Diary,

After a breakfast of untoasted toast eaten over the wastebasket to avoid getting any dishes dirty, Dad dropped me off at school early today. Angeline was there already, taping up some of her posters. I decided to give her some helpful pointers.

"These are horrible," I helpfully pointed out. "What are you doing?"

"I'm putting up some posters," she said simply.

I shook my head. "This is **vertical littering**. Take these down. I'll make the posters you need."

Angeline said that even after our conversation yesterday, she wasn't sure that I understood bullying.

BE NICE TO EVERYBODY

Angeline's ANTI-BULLYING POSTERS KIND OF MADE ME **WANT TO** BULLY Some kid.

"Yes, I do. It's about not being mean to people. Not saying mean things to them. Not calling them bad names. It's not that hard, Angeline. You think I can't see it because Isabella is my best friend, right?"

"Isabella is a bully," Angeline said.

"And that's a **bad thing**?" I asked.

"Of course it's bad!"

"Not the kind of thing you'd want to be called, right?"

Angeline saw where I was going.

"I don't think you should call her that anymore," I said. "Isabella has a lot of things going for her."

If you hurt a BULLY's feelings, aren't YOU a bully?

Imagine Poor Isabella so depressed that she hardly wants to punch everybody.

"Isabella makes fun of how people speak," Angeline said.

"Isabella gives free speech therapy," I replied.

"Isabella takes people's lunches."

"Isabella teaches people how to share," I said.

"Isabella is mean to her very best friend, the one human being on Earth who stands up for her no matter how mean she is. **EVERY. SINGLE. DAY.**"

I didn't have a response for this.

"I have a perfect response for this," I said, "but I don't have time. I have to go to class."

Angeline wasn't having it. She grabbed my arm and dragged me into the office, past the front desk, and to the doorway of Assistant Principal Devon's office (who, I may have mentioned before, is Angeline's uncle and also mine).

"Jamie and I would like to miss our first classes so that we can work on some stuff. Okay?"

"You got it. I'll let your teachers know," Assistant Principal Devon said.

There are people who benefit from rules, and people who are punished by rules, and then there are people like Angeline, who don't really seem to notice them at all, and the rules seem **okay with that**.

I looked at her in disbelief as we walked away from the office. "Will he let you do that anytime you ask? Skip a class?"

"If I have a good reason, he will," she said.

"But he didn't even know the reason," I pointed out.

"He doesn't need to. He knows it's good."

We went down to Miss Anderson's classroom to see if she'd let us make posters, and she said okay, but she made me use the **cheap glitter**. She knew I was making them for the Student Awareness Committee, and not the Cuisine Club.

Here's what I came up with:

HIS WAY TO THE AWESOME POSTERS...

GLITTER

C'MON TURN THE PAGE

48

THURSDAY 12

Dear Dumb Diary,

Today at lunch, Miss Anderson really went out of her way for the membership drive.

It's a well-known fact that the fragrance of fresh popcorn can reduce a hungry person to insanity, and she was handing out little bags of it at the entrance to the lunchroom. On each bag, she had written **THE CUISINE CLUB. JOIN NOW. MEETS EVERY WEDNESDAY.**

She was even dressed as an adorable bag of popcorn that might also dance in a show in Las Vegas, and she was mobbed by kids (and stared at by that one janitor who is evidently also way into popcorn).

Her promotion was a huge success. Isabella even took a bag.

A BAG.

ONE BAG.

I asked Isabella why she took only one, and she looked at me, a little dazed.

"My brothers moved out. When I got home yesterday, they were already gone. They got jobs at a theme park — and they'll be living there."

"Did your parents know this was coming?"

"Yeah. My dad said that since they've graduated from high school and they're not sure about college, they can't just lie around, and this is as good a plan as any. **They're gone.** Gone forever."

"Are you going to miss them?"

"Jamie," she said, "I've been throwing snowballs, rocks, and bricks at those two for as long as I can remember. I never missed them once, and I don't think I'll start missing them now."

Aww! Baby Isabella! Cute and Dangerous.
Like a COBRA iN a Diaper.

Angeline was looking over at Miss Anderson's popcorn triumph, and she seemed so deflated that I went to talk to her about kids doing terrible things to each other, you know, because I thought that might help to cheer her up.

"Hey, Angeline," I said, trying to sound positive. "I'll bet our posters really made an impact on kids, even though I know the whole point is for kids to **not** feel impacts. Heh, heh," I said, adding, "Heh, heh."

She sighed. "Yeah, and I know that's what matters. But you know this little popcorn performance by Miss Anderson is going to tip the numbers in your favor. The Cuisine Club will win the membership drive."

I asked how she could know that, and she reminded me that she's the one who collects the club information and reports it all to Assistant Principal Uncle Dan. She knows the numbers.

"I think you guys may have won by just a kid or two," she said sadly. "It's over."

This is what one of these looks like when all the perky leaks out of it.

"So what? Nobody cares about that," I said, caring deeply.

"It's a **cash prize**, Jamie. The club that wins gets a cash prize to make their club better. I know you and Isabella don't care about the club we started together, but I do."

I felt bad.

I wonder if Angeline making me feel bad is a form of bullying. I think it is.

She should feel bad about **that**.

If you make me feel guilty, you're going to feel BAD that you did.

And then **I'M** going to feel BAD that I made you feel BAD.

Then you'll feel bad, then I'll feel bad, then you'll feel bad.

We'll **ALL** feel much better if I never feel guilty.

FRIDAY 13

Dear Dumb Diary,

.We're out of bread, so we couldn't have Dad's famous untoasted toast today.

So he came up with something new — Astronaut Cereal. He introduced the idea to me in one of those high voices that work on you when you're two years old and never again.

"Look, Jamie!" he said shrilly. "Put the cereal in a plastic bag! Then pour the milk right in!" He showed me what he meant. "Then mash it up! Now, cut a hole in the corner of the bag and suck it right out of there like an astronaut!"

I imagined that if the entire space program did things this dumb, we would have to walk around **looking up** all the time to make sure those morons didn't drop a wrench on us from space.

OMG
MAKE
IT
STOP
OMG
OMG
OMG
OMG

By the time we got to school, my breakfast was sucked. (That sounds accurate in more ways than one.)

Isabella and Angeline were waiting at my locker.

"The numbers are in," Angeline said.

"The Cuisine Club is going to win?" I asked, being politely not too happy.

"Nope."

"The Student Awareness Committee?"

"Nope."

"So, it was the Videogamer Club."

"Nope."

"Then who's going to win?" I squawked — but, you know, femininely.

I can even burp femininely.

It sounds like a fairy squeezing a teensy bicycle horn.

"It's a three-way tie," Angeline announced.

"So, none of us can win?" I asked.

Angeline grinned. "We can split the money three ways."

"Yeah," I said. "I guess. Let's do that, you know, if you're telling me that there's no other choice."

"Wllthrzwunothrstdnt," Angeline mumbled.

"Did you say something?" Isabella said.

"Wllthrzwunothrstdnt," Angeline mumbled again, this time a bit louder.

I grabbed her by her shoulders and gave her a shake until she blurted out the truth.

"I said that there is one other student that hasn't joined any club on Wednesdays. Well, one that anybody would want, anyway, but I don't see why we can't just split the money instead of competing for that one last person."

I looked at Isabella. She smiled, and I was pretty sure I knew why.

"Okay, Angeline," I said. "You're right. Let's split it. But **just out of curiosity**, who is that last student?"

Shaking the truth out of a blond is just like making a beagle drop a chicken bone.

She told us.

It's Dicky Flartsnutt.

Dicky Flartsnutt. Sometimes you get the feeling that a kid's parents named them just hoping that they'd get tormented for the rest of their lives.

Dicky is shorter than he needs to be, wider than he needs to be, a wearer of glasses, braces, and prescription socks.

He's sensitive to perfumes, and allergic to peanuts, shellfish, strawberries, artificial colors, artificial flavors, wood, vinyl, and somehow, the number five.

He isn't very good at sports, the arts, or school, and he doesn't seem to have a single friend.

He lisps, bites his nails, doesn't comb his hair, and always seems to run into things.

But he always seems to be in a **good mood**.

EAR LUBRICANT. WHAT IS THAT? NOBODY KNOWS.

BIZARRE OPTIMISM →

PANTS STOLEN OFF DEAD CLOWN? WE HAVE NO REAL PROOF.

BAND-AIDS IN PLACES NOBODY EVER GETS INJURED.

YES. IT'S A DUCKY.

SHOES SMELL LIKE INFLATABLE BABY POOL.

I smiled, and Angeline smiled back.

And then it suddenly occurred to her why I was smiling, and she gasped.

"You're going after him," she wheezed.

"Sorry, Angeline. My loyalty lies with the Cuisine Club. Stop by sometime, and I'll teach you something about *how the cookie crumbles*." And I made a supercool face at her and shouted, **"WHOAAAAA!"** Really cool. I don't know how else to describe it. Just supercool. Really supercool.

"What's that supposed to mean?" she said.

"Like the saying. You know: *That's how the cookie crumbles*. You've heard that saying," I said.

"That's just ignorant," she said, and walked away. And she kind of wrecked my cool face, and made my **WHOAAAAA** seem unimportant.

"You've heard that saying before, haven't you, Isabella?" I asked the air where Isabella had been standing.

She was gone.

"FLARTSNUTT!" I hissed, and ran all the way to Dicky's locker.

I rounded the corner and Isabella was there, but the entire area was **Flartsnuttless**.

"So. I see how it is," I said to her.

Isabella shrugged. "My club needs games. They're expensive. Controllers and consoles cost a lot of money. What does your little club need? Flour? Salt?"

I tried a different approach. "Isabella, let's work together on this. Help me get Flartsnutt in the Cuisine Club, and I'll talk Miss Anderson into buying your club a game."

"Sorry, Jamie. I work alone. You know that," she said, and I was absolutely shocked.

Isabella had said **"sorry."**

— *How she usually uses it* —

SATURDAY 14

Dear Dumb Diary,

Dad woke me up today, very early, in a panic. He had a laundry basket with him.

"Do we have one of those machines that cleans things made out of cloth?" he shouted. Evidently, the concept of laundry had just occurred to him.

I was pretty groggy, and my voice sounded like an old door opening.

"A washing machine? Yes. Of course we do. In the basement," I creaked.

"Well, these things are dirty and your mother is coming home."

"When?" I said, sitting up. "When is Mom coming home?"

"**Eventually!**" he said, and I heard him run all the way down to the basement with the laundry basket.

I showed Dad how to separate the items by color, how to put in the detergent, and how to choose the settings on the washing machine.

He studied the jug of detergent.

"Huh. They make a special soap just for cloth. Did you know that, Jamie?" he said. "They should do that for the dishes, too."

He was genuinely impressed at how much I knew, and I was genuinely surprised at how much he **didn't**.

"Dad, what if you had never met Mom? How would you take care of yourself?" I asked.

"I'd live in a box," he said sadly, looking off into the distance. "A dirty, dirty box. With my daughter and her two beagles. Except we might have to eat the beagles."

I laughed.

But **NOT** off of plates. We wouldn't want to get any plates dirty.

After I finished with Dad, I could resume **Operation Flartsnutt**, which is now in full effect. It shouldn't be hard to get him to join the Cuisine Club — everybody likes food, but not everybody likes video games or awareness.

I figured that my dad is probably a former wad, because he still retains many **wadlike** traits, and therefore he might be able to provide some insight as to what a wad like Dicky might like.

"Dad. You were a wad, right?" I asked sweetly.

He raised an eyebrow. "No. Why do you ask?"

"I was thinking of trying out a few menu items on you to see if they're the sorts of things that wads like. I'll clean up any mess I make, and all you have to do is eat."

"You'll clean up EVERYTHING?" he asked nervously.

"Yes."

"Will these food objects contain some sort of dead animal?"

"Meat? Yes, Dad. There will be meat."

He smiled. "You may proceed to feed the wad."

Dad is a great Guinea Pig. I think he would even eat a Guinea Pig.

I prepared the following items and got Dad's reaction. I had to work quickly, because I figured that Isabella might start pounding on the door any minute and begin eating everything I made, but she never did.

She must be enjoying some brotherless time at home.

FOOD ITEM		DAD'S REACTION
cheese with pickle on toast		
Salami and ketchup on cucumber slice		
Dog food and toenail on piece of paper		
Salami with cheese and mustard on cracker with tomato sliver.		

As you can see, the salami-and-cheese crackers with a dab of mustard and sliver of tomato got very high marks from Dad. These will be easy to make and transport to school on Monday.

And when Dicky wraps his plump, chapped lips around one of these babies, the contest will be in the bag.

NERDS — THANK YOU FOR TRYING TO BE LESS UNATTRACTIVE WHEN EATING

SUNDAY 15

Dear Dumb Diary,

    Angeline and Aunt Carol showed up at my house this morning and offered to take me to the mall.

    When they showed up, Dad was trying to get me to eat a raw egg for breakfast so we wouldn't get a pan dirty. His idea was to poke a hole in it with a pen, and drink the contents with a straw. That way, we could throw away the straw and wipe the pen clean on the grass.

    So I had to decide between Angeline and **food poisoning**. I know what you're thinking, Dumb Diary, it really shouldn't have been a difficult choice. You're right, but I chose Angeline anyway.

C'mon, Jamie! Snakes and weasels **LOVE** them this way!

We walked around the mall for a bit, asking each other which things were **cute** and which things were **not cute**. Mom and I can never take Dad shopping, because he can't understand why we need to discuss these things and usually don't even buy anything. Dad wrongly believes that shopping always involves actual shopping.

At one point, Angeline and Aunt Carol wanted to go look at sandals and I wasn't feeling it, so I just sat on a bench and judged the people that walked by.

I know that people don't deserve to be judged just for walking through a mall, but I offer the service to them **free of charge** anyway.

DRESSES TOO YOUNG FOR HER AGE

UGLY SHIRT

HEY THAT'S MY SHIRT

JACKET TOO SMALL, ALSO HEAD

A BOWTIE? REALLY? ARE YOU MY WAITER?

AWESOME SHIRT, WEIRDO LADY

I had just finished determining that one person's ensemble would be perfect for butchering chickens and then hurling into a volcano, when I noticed an exchange taking place over at another bench.

It was **Dicky Flartsnutt**. He was sitting on the bench while Butch Dirggen and two of his friends were standing there, talking to him.

Butch is the only kid in Mackerel Middle School who can almost grow a mustache, unless you count that kid who drinks chocolate milk all the time, and that just **looks** like one.

Butch is big, and mean, and always in trouble. Most kids just stay out of his way.

SEMI-MUSTACHEY

chocolate mustache

BUTCH

Also a stylish ketchup beard

I wasn't sure I wanted to go over and talk to Dicky with Butch and his friends there, but fortunately, one of them grabbed Dicky's hat and they all ran away with it. (I've noticed that bullies have a **far-above-average** interest in hats.)

He watched them run away, and then sat there with his head down. It was a perfect time to begin my recruitment.

I walked over and sat down.

"It's Dicky, right?" I said. "We go to the same school."

He looked up cautiously and when he saw me, smiled slightly.

"Oh, hi," he said. "Yeah. I know you. Of course I know you."

How could he **NOT** know me, right? I'm pretty well-known for my posters and dancing and prettiness. Many things, really. Too many to count. A million, let's say.

"You're Angeline's friend."

Bullies have some kind of weird HAT-LOVE

I smiled and corrected him.

"Angeline is *my* friend," I said, noting how bad that sentence tasted in my mouth, like a pink jelly bean that you might find in the bottom of a discarded aquarium.

"Did Butch steal your hat?" I asked.

"Oh, no. He's just borrowing it. He borrows it sometimes, but he always returns it later."

"He's going to return it?"

Dicky nodded. "Yes. For sure. I just never know *where* he'll return it. Sometimes he returns it on the roof of the school. One time, he returned it to his dog."

I nodded.

"It has my name in it. I'll find it."

I noticed that many of the things he was wearing had his name on them.

"Listen, Dicky," I said. "I'm making some snack-type things for the Cuisine Club, and I'm supposed to get some kids' opinions on them. Would it be okay if we had lunch together tomorrow and you gave them a try?"

Dicky just sat and stared at me as if he hadn't heard me.

"Dicky?"

"This is just so amazing," he said.

I laughed that off, but it was really kind of **tragic**. I mean, of course he should have been flattered I offered to join him and everything, but c'mon, Dicky, it's not like I'm the most beautiful girl in the ~~school~~ world.

Oh, Dicky
The word
GORGEOUS
is just
SO
OVERUSED.

And yet, I understand why you really don't have a choice sometimes.

I returned to my bench, and Dicky's mom came and picked him up. They were gone before Angeline and Aunt Carol got back. It had worked out perfectly.

"Did you see anything cute?" I asked.

Aunt Carol shook her head. "We saw two things that were cute but also kind of bleh, and one thing that was cuteish but also kind of I don't know."

I had a perfect picture in my mind of what they saw, and I suddenly felt a little sorry for Dad that he would **never understand** what we were talking about.

Oh, Dad. What you don't know . . .

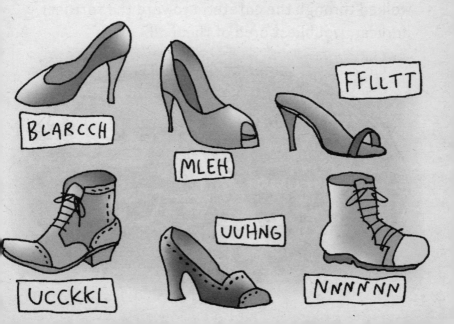

BLARCCH

MLEH

FFLLTT

UCCKKL

UUHNG

NNNNNN

MONDAY 16

Dear Dumb Diary,

In most cafeterias, there are zones. There are territories. There are little kingdoms of joy and attractiveness, little villages of pleasantness, and little quiet areas that seem a bit unpopulated and underdeveloped.

Way, way past these areas, there are **dark corners**. Bleak, lonely, isolated spots, where the wobbliest chairs and tables eventually wind up.

Dicky's words suddenly came back to me as I walked through the cafeteria toward the farthest, darkest, wobbliest area of them all.

WOBBLY CHAIRS
BROKEN LIGHTS
DIRTY FLOORS
NERD ODOR

I had my little Tupperware container of fabulous snacks in my hand, and I heard his scratchy voice in my head.

"This is just so amazing," he had said.

And I saw *why* Dicky thought it was all so amazing.

I wasn't the only one who had made arrangements to have lunch with Dicky today.

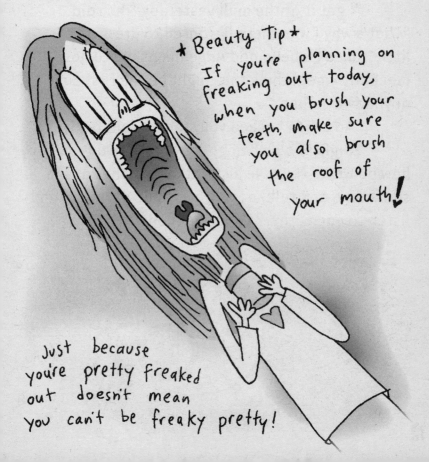

Beauty Tip
If you're planning on freaking out today, when you brush your teeth, make sure you also brush the roof of your mouth!

Just because you're pretty freaked out doesn't mean you can't be freaky pretty!

Angeline and Isabella were sitting next to him.

"Oh, hi," Angeline said frigidly.

Isabella just nodded.

"Hi, Jamie," Dicky said merrily. It looked like he had tried combing his hair, and he was wearing a new shirt. I can tell things like that.

"You left the price tag on your shirt, Dicky," I said, and he pulled it off with a snap.

"I got it at the mall yesterday," he said. "That's why I was there. I wanted to dress up a little, since Isabella and Angeline asked to have lunch with me. I think this might be the first time anybody ever has."

"And then I asked you, too," I said flatly.

"Right! So amazing!" he said with a grin. "So, how do we do this? We just eat our lunches at the same time and talk, or do we eat one at a time and listen to each other? I've never done this."

I don't know

How to Lunch

74

Isabella pulled out her phone and launched a game. She wasn't wasting any time.

"You like video games?" she asked Dicky.

"I don't know," he said, chewing on a mouthful of what looked like a hay sandwich.

"Well, you've played them, right?" she said.

"No. Was I supposed to?"

Isabella scowled. I mean, how does a person answer a question like that?

"Yes," she answered. "You were supposed to."

Dicky took a sip of a juice box that had a picture of a cabbage on it.

"Okay. Show me," he said.

prescription sandwich

prescription gross items

"Look. This one is called **Zombie Spanker**. You have to spank all the zombies that are coming at you," Isabella explained. "See, tap here to spank them."

"Oh, cool!" Dicky said. "Let's run away from them."

"No. Dicky. Look. We *spank* the zombies. See? Spank 'em."

"But they're people," Dicky said.

"Yeah, once, but now they're infected with zombie virus. We have to spank 'em."

"I'll bet we can get them a doctor," Dicky said, examining the screen closely for a **CALL A DOCTOR** button.

Isabella took the phone away from him. "Let me find a different game."

Angeline wedged herself in.

"Dicky, we're in a club here called the Student Awareness Committee, and right now we're doing something to increase awareness about bullying."

Dicky opened a little sandwich bag of leaflike things to snack on. They could have been kale. They could have been triangles of green felt.

"Did you ever have any experience with bullies?" Angeline went on, making her voice sound all sincere and junk, because she was.

"I guess so," Dicky said. "Like Butch and his friends."

"And don't you think we should put an end to it?"

"That depends," Dicky lisped.

"On what?" Angeline said.

"Well, are you guys going to talk to me from now on?" he asked.

Angeline looked surprised. "Why would that matter?"

"Because Butch and his friends are the only people that talk to me. I'm not sure I would want that to stop completely."

Not what Angeline was going for.

My turn.

"Dicky," I said, "What Isabella and Angeline were doing here to make you uncomfortable was really great — wonderful stuff, ladies — but you'll remember that the reason that *I* suggested we dine together was so that you could try these."

I opened the Tupperware container, and somehow the fragrance was even better than I expected. It smelled like somebody had opened a **decanter of love**, if love is made out of salami, as I think most of us suspect that it is.

I took out a perfect little meaty, cheesy appetizer, and held it up so that the small amount of light that managed to make it into this region of the lunchroom through the window danced on the cracker's salt crystals.

"I made this," I whispered. "We can teach you to make them, too."

"It's beautiful," he said. "But I can tell just from looking at it that I can't eat at least three of the things it's made of."

I could be a food-holding model in cookbooks.

So **Project Flartsnutt** isn't off to a great start. It wasn't a total loss. I gave Dad the rest of the snacks that night, and he was really happy that we could eat dinner directly out of a Tupperware container that I told him I would clean.

"See, Jamie," he said, "if you eat directly over the dustpan, you don't have to get a broom dirty sweeping up."

FROM THE LUNATIC DAD that brought you EATING OVER A DUSTPAN

Why not try HAVING OVER THE TOILET TO KEEP THE SINK CLEAN?

TUESDAY 17

Dear Dumb Diary,

Today in science with Mrs. Curie, we had to watch some gruesome real-life nature thing about some hyenas playing a little too rough with their friend, the wildebeest, by trying to eat it alive. It made me wonder why people are always trying to protect Nature, because very often Nature is a huge jerk.

It honestly made me consider not recycling anymore, just to get back at Nature.

Eventually, some other wildebeests came charging in to the rescue and scared off the hyenas, which was a relief, but I couldn't help thinking: Hey, wildebeests, what took you so long? You have something else to do? Checking your email or something?

PROTECTING YOUR SPECIES is, like, one of the two jobs you have. It's just that, and eating those clumps of dry, nasty grass you seem to enjoy.

And hey, antelopes, I'm looking at you, too.

We were almost all the way through lunch today when I realized that I hadn't even said hi to Dicky. He was probably way back in the far corner of the lunchroom, wondering why his two new pretty friends and the blond hadn't even said hello.

I started to suggest it to Isabella but when I looked at her, she was reading a note that she'd found in with her lunch, and smiling.

"What's that?" I asked her.

"A note from my dad. He packed my lunch today and put a note in it. He's never done that before."

Isabella got up and emptied her tray in the trash. As she walked away, I saw her put the note in her pocket.

Angeline leaned in and whispered, "It's because her brothers are gone, you know. She's kind of smoothing out."

OMG.
ISABELLA.
READ.
VOLUNTARILY.

It's a weird new world.

WEDNESDAY 18

Dear Dumb Diary,

    I haven't really been writing much about my classes lately, because I've been so focused on the whole club situation. Quick update:
    In English today, I told Mrs. Avon that it made sense to me that the word **NOUN** was a noun, but shouldn't the word **VERB** be a verb?
    Yeah, okay. Not that interesting. You see? This is why I've been telling you about the clubs.

School is responsible for 67% of the World's drool.

Miss Anderson was in a pretty bad mood during the Cuisine Club today. We increased the number of kids in the club, but now we have **too many**.

We made vegetable appetizers, but it was five people to a carrot and we had to split the toothpicks.

Miss Anderson told us that we were fine as a tiny club, but with all these new kids, we have to win this membership drive to get the extra funds. There's no in-between size for us. Without the win, she's going to have to cancel the club due to overcrowding.

And then she brought out the dessert, like a big hunk of bait. She said she HOPED we would get to make it IF we get enough people to join the club.

You could actually hear some of the stomachs knot up at the prospect of eating her cake, mine included. Dad's meals just aren't keeping me going.

pure deliciousness

For example, Dad made dinner tonight. It was hotdogs, but they were not in buns and not on plates and not cooked and did not have condiments.

He calls them **notdogs**.

After dinner, I called Isabella to tell her this, and when she got on the phone she was already laughing.

LAUGHING.

"Isabella," I said, thinking quickly, "if you're being held hostage right now and are just laughing to confuse whoever it is that's got you, say our code word, which I suddenly realize we never agreed to, but let's say now that the code word is **'hostage.'**"

Isabella said everything was fine. Her mom had just said something funny and she and her dad were laughing about it.

"What's up?" she asked, and for just a moment she sounded all bright and cheery, like Angeline. I felt like my **notdog** was **notsittingwell**.

"Nobody can know that Dicky is the one remaining student that can win it for our clubs. He can't take the attention. He already bought one new shirt this year and —"

"Okay," Isabella said.

"What? No argument? No pushback?"

"Sounds good, Jamie. See you tomorrow."

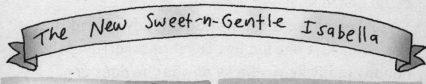

The New Sweet-n-Gentle Isabella

Will no longer strangle counter people for getting her order wrong.

Won't kick the TV during car insurance commercials.

Will stop screaming at birds for singing too early.

Give me a break. Even I kick the TV during car insurance commercials.

Dear Dumb Diary,

We have to be very careful about giving Dicky the rush. If anybody notices what we're doing, it could be trouble.

Somehow, the news had already spread that there was just one kid left to recruit. Fortunately, nobody really knows Dicky or what he does or doesn't do.

Even so, Isabella, Angeline, and I were really casual today when we went over to his table. We were all like, "Oh, we hardly noticed you sitting over in this dank, abandoned part of the cafeteria on the terrible chairs. Maybe we'll just sit down here casually and casually talk casually, you know, not about anything in particular."

"Join my club," Isabella said.

"Club?" Dicky said.

I jumped in.

I can say things so casually that even I don't know what I'm talking about.

"Look, Dicky, what Isabella is trying to say here is that you should join the Cuisine Club. We can teach you how to make better lunches than whatever that is you're eating."

I pointed at a little container that appeared to have a **lab specimen** in it.

"It's a beet pudding," he said.

Angeline was getting ready to make her pitch when Butch and his friends showed up.

ASSISTANT BULLIES, I GUESS

"Is this guy bothering you, ladies?" he said, trying to be charming by jiggling his big fat hairy eyebrows up and down. You know, the way that charming guys do.

"No," Angeline said. "Thanks, anyway."

Butch wasn't giving up. "Because sometimes his lunches make people sick just to look at. That's why he knows he has to eat them back here where nobody has to see their nastiness."

Dicky smiled. "I guess that's reasonable," he said.

"Hey, guys, why don't you just leave us alone," I said, which turned out to be **fairly unwise**.

"Why don't you make us?" Butch asked. Isabella turned around in her chair and looked up at him. His smirk changed quickly when he realized that it was Isabella he had been standing behind.

"It's kind of a private conversation we're having," she said, smiling. It was the smile of a girl no longer pestered every day by her brothers. It was the smile of a girl at peace. It was the smile of a girl who wanted to communicate like a human being.

Later, when I was helping Angeline get the beet pudding out of her hair in the girls' bathroom, I asked Isabella why she didn't just push Butch's face down his throat.

"I don't know," she said, pulling the piece of kale out of her ear that Butch had stuffed inside it. "Does that really solve anything?"

After we cleaned up, we headed down to the office. Assistant Principal Devon was expecting us.

When we got there, Assistant Principal Devon was talking to Dicky. The school nurse had put a Band-Aid on his cheek and offered to call his parents. Butch and his friends slumped in chairs nearby.

"I'm fine," Dicky said. "I slipped on some organic cabbage juice. Butch caught me. Angeline, Isabella, and Jamie saw it all."

He looked at us with the **Universal Eyes of Lying**, which all kids recognize.

"That how it happened?" Assistant Principal Devon asked us, asking Angeline a little bit more than me and Isabella.

Who knew?

Nerds Lie.

Butch and his friends looked over at us. I could see some real concern in their eyes, especially Butch's. He was nervously picking kale from underneath his fingernails.

"Do you think Dicky's a liar?" Angeline asked Assistant Principal Uncle Dan, now putting him in the position of having to say something terrible about Dicky, who already had things pretty rough, and who **could** have been telling the truth.

PLUS, you clever blond devil, you didn't actually lie, yourself, did you?

Suddenly I think Angeline might be good at chess

pretty, pretty chess

Assistant Principal Devon smiled at us, but it wasn't a real smile.

"No. Of course not," he said. "We just don't want to see accidents like this happen. Back to class, everyone."

Assistant Principal Smiles

SO PROUD OF YOU FOR BRINGING THAT E UP TO A D—

CAN'T WAIT TO SIT THROUGH ANOTHER SCHOOL MUSICAL

YES, MRS. WHATEVER, PLEASE TELL ME WHAT SCHOOLS DO WRONG

OH. IT'S FRIDAY ALREADY? INTERESTING.

FRIDAY 20

Dear Dumb Diary,

Today, Angeline and some of the recent additions to the Student Awareness Committee had set up a table in the school lobby and were asking people to sign a pledge not to bully.

I signed it, of course, because it's the right thing to do. Plus I have a **lovely signature**, which I'm always prepared to share with people.

Isabella is also prepared to share her signature, but in the past it's always been with spray paint, at night, not her real signature, and there's typically a pretty gross drawing accompanying it.

NAILS AS LOVELY AS A CASHIER'S →

Jamie Kelly

PRICELESS BRACELET FROM MOVIE STAR OR FIREMAN

Of course, Butch had to wander in because, well, it looks like now he's part of our lives.

"What's this?" he asked, fumbling at the clipboard with his big fat hairy fingers and staring at it with his big fat hairy eyes.

"It's a pledge not to bully," Angeline said. "Sign it."

He read down the list of names.

"Isabella? Isabella signed this?" He laughed. "Oh, man. She really is going **soft**."

He flipped the clipboard back to Angeline.

"**YOU** sign it," he said, and laughed again, mistaking what he had just said as a clever comeback.

Isabella going soft? Yeah, right.

A soft Isabella would be so sweet!

Although Not sure I could fall asleep with it in my room.

We all had another go at Dicky today. Isabella had a new game — a racing game — and Dicky was concerned that they might be exceeding the speed limit. Angeline's pitch was about more of the things we should be aware of, like recycling and conservation and stuff, but Dicky said he thought that everybody was already aware of those things but just chose to **ignore** them.

I had a carefully prepared appetizer of organic gluten-free soy something on top of a low-sodium peanut-free something else — I don't know, Stinker wouldn't even eat it — and Dicky enjoyed it, but said it seemed like an awful lot of work to make something so beautiful that you're just going to chew up and swallow.

He wasn't wrong.

Just as lunch was ending, we got up to leave and passed Butch, who angled his shoulder in such a way as to bump Isabella's shoulder.

She just rolled with it and kept walking. I looked back and saw Butch smile.

I'm afraid that he was conducting a test, and Isabella had failed.

"You're supposed to say **'sorry'** when you run into somebody, Isabella. You're not trying to bully me or something, are you?" Butch yelled after her.

Isabella turned, and Dicky stepped in between them, effectively distracting them both from their bubbling conflict.

"Isabella, how about if you and Angeline and Jamie come over to my house tomorrow, and we can talk about which club I should join."

I'm going, but I know I'm going to **hate** this.

SATURDAY 21

Dear Dumb Diary,

    Dicky only lives a couple streets away from me, so after a hearty breakfast of Bunny Bananas, which is the "fun name" Dad came up with for carrots wrapped in paper towels, I swung by Isabella's house and we walked over. Angeline's mom was dropping her off as we arrived.

    Dicky's house had flamingos and garden gnomes out front. It had a silly welcome mat and a sign on the door that said, *The Flartsnutts Welcome You*. Next to the door was a pot with a plant that had died so long ago it may have technically qualified as a fossil.

⭐ *Dad's other Kitchen Creations* ⭐

THE LOLLYSPUD — POTATO ON DISPOSABLE FORK

SUSHI ROBOT — CAN OF TUNA FISH

MAGIC FOOD GLITTER SPRINKLES — SALT (USE ON LOLLYSPUD)

We rang the bell, and Dicky came to the door.

"Your plant's dead," Isabella said in greeting.

"Mom's hoping it will come back," Dicky explained cheerfully. "It's been like that for six years, but Mom is really optimistic. Sometimes she talks to it."

"Does that help?" I asked.

"It doesn't seem to hurt it," Dicky replied.

A friendly little dog came up wagging his tail, and with him, a friendly little cat.

A friendly little dad came to the door next, with a friendly little mom and a friendly little sister.

"Dicky's told us all about you," his mom said. "Angeline, I know that you're quite sweet and smart and a very good friend to Jamie, although Jamie doesn't always know it. Isabella, I know that you're tough and very clever, and not afraid of anything. Jamie, I know that you're very creative and artistic and that you feel things deeply. Did I get that right?"

"What are you?" Isabella said. "Some kind of fortune-teller?"

OH, HI THERE....

...BELLADONNA...

..ISADORA...

..ELISSA BELLA.

.. ISAAC NEWTON...

...IBBLE DIBBLE...

..EBOLA...

OMG. MY DAD CAN'T EVEN GET ISABELLA'S NAME RIGHT.

At lunch, we learned that the Flartsnutts laughed at **everything**. Not idiotic laughter, just free, easy, happy laughter.

Eventually we started laughing, too, and soon we were all laughing so hard that the horrible food that Dicky eats actually started to seem kind of good, as if eating something through a smile makes it taste better somehow.

His mom and dad and little sister knew everything about his teachers, the school, his hobbies — **everything**.

And when these people spoke to each other, the love was deafening. It was enormous. I never knew a family could be like this. I mean, my parents love me and everything, but c'mon, there's a limit, right? I ached for a sister, and a cat, and a dog. Okay, I have dogs, but I ached for nicer ones.

Isabella was quiet most of the time, until we started to talk to Dicky's family about our clubs. Isabella told them about video games, and Dicky's dad said he had heard that they improved reflexes in doctors and pilots who played them regularly, but he didn't think they needed to be as violent as they were.

Then Angeline talked about the Student Awareness Committee, and Dicky's mom told us about the huge amount of volunteer work they do as a family, and how everything begins with awareness.

I told them about the Cuisine Club, too, and everyone agreed that it was fun to make beautiful things to eat. Dicky's mom even said maybe I could give her some tips sometime.

After lunch, we played a board game and the time flew by. When it was time to go, we thanked them — and in a weird way, I think I saw Dicky differently.

Dicky wears an armor made of pure love. The reason why things don't get to him is that he drinks up so much love at home that he never runs out. Dicky is a **love camel**.

When he said good-bye to us, he apologized for having only one Wednesday to offer, because he felt bad that he couldn't join all three clubs.

I felt a little ashamed of myself walking home.

"I didn't know a family could be like that," Isabella said quietly. "I didn't know that they could be that . . . *nice* to each other."

SUNDAY 22

Dear Dumb Diary,

Angeline called this morning and begged for help with more posters. I wasn't really up for it, but after seeing how nice Dicky and his family are, it sort of made me feel **nicer**. Like, I really didn't have anything against Angeline, and she did offer to bring some extra glitter.

I really can't overemphasize the significance of glitter in everything. While you're young, you use a lot of it because of its powerful natural beauty. When you reach my age, glitter really sends a message that you put in the extra time. Glitter becomes the code for commitment. I firmly believe that when a law is really important, they should write it in glitter.

THIS SERIOUS LAW IS SO IMPORTANT THAT IT NEEDS SOME MAGENTA GLITTER

AND ALSO SOME STRAWBERRY-KIWI BODY SPLASH.

Once Angeline showed up, we started right in. I had a few ideas about healthy-eating awareness, because Dicky's awful food had made me aware that horrible things are good.

Or something like that . . . I don't know . . . look, awareness doesn't happen all at once. I need some time to figure out how to spin this.

Angeline was still all about the bullying issue. She got a little intense about it, and I finally asked her why this was such a big deal for her, anyway. Wasn't it time to be aware of something else already?

"It's not like you ever get bullied," I said.

She looked at me sadly.

"No, but I **am** one," she answered.

Honestly, Angeline. I'm supposed to BELIEVE THIS?

SQUEAK

"I'm as bad as Isabella," Angeline went on. "I judge people without knowing them. I laugh when I think somebody is funny looking or dumb. I may even sometimes think less of people for things they can't help. Sometimes I even resent people who are nicer than me, or more talented, or prettier. How awful is that?"

"You should never resent somebody for being prettier," I said sternly. "I can't help it, Angeline."

Angeline sighed. "If I feel this way about people, Jamie, I'm *almost* a bully."

I wanted to console her.

"You are a bad person," I said.

I wasn't done. "But you're not a bully. You're allowed to *think* anything you want, and I don't believe we can keep ourselves from laughing at certain things. I mean, I really like Dicky, but I am **never** going to be okay with those shoes of his."

Angeline tried not to laugh.

"I think it's about keeping your big fat hairy mouth shut, and keeping your big fat hairy hands to yourself. And if you **DO** feel the irresistible need to discuss the dumbness of Dicky Flartsnutt's shoes, you had better make sure it doesn't get back to him — because if it does, even accidentally, and he feels bad about it, you might have become a kind of bully."

"Those shoes are made out of the same thing they make pencil erasers from," Angeline blurted, and then covered her mouth as if she had actually spoken a fart.

"I'm telling him you said that," I said seriously. Angeline looked terribly upset for a moment before laughing.

"Did you ever say anything mean about me?" she asked.

I stopped and thought for a moment. "Nope," I said.

MONDAY 23

Dear Dumb Diary,

Just before school today, Isabella and I spotted Dicky outside. I was happy to see that he had gotten his hat back.

For some reason, it was in the branches of a tree by the front entrance.

"How did that get up there?" I asked.

"Oh, just an accident, I guess," Dicky said.

"I threw it up there," Butch said, walking up to join us in a big fat hairy manner.

Isabella looked at him for a **long moment**, and then up at the hat. I had seen her do this sort of calculation in her head before. I knew she was trying to determine how many times she would have to pound Butch's head against the trunk to shake the hat loose, and if he would lose consciousness in the process.

↑
HAT

"I always hated that hat," Dicky said, and walked inside.

Butch laughed **bigly** and **hairily** and walked away **fatly**.

I looked at Isabella, and she just shrugged.

"I guess Dicky hates the hat," she said. "All's well that ends well." As we headed into school, I thought about how great it was that Isabella had come so far so quickly.

I wonder if her brothers have changed without her. I'm so glad they're never coming back.

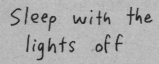
Things they can do without Isabella around

Not keep their snacks locked in a trunk

Sleep with the lights off

Not keep Isabella locked in a trunk

TUESDAY 24

Dear Dumb Diary,

    I thought that nobody could be more pleased about Isabella's newly developed niceness than me. But today, I think I discovered one person who's even happier about her change:

Butch.

    Butch sat down at our lunch table today. He stared right into Isabella's eyes, reached over, and grabbed a chip off her tray. A good chip. A *barbecue* chip.

    Six chairs immediately pushed away from the table. I was not about to get cabbage-juiced again.

    But Isabella did nothing. She just kept eating. This was the new Isabella — calmer, gentler, more in control of her temper.

    Then Butch reached for something on Dicky's tray.

There was a blur of motion, a loud snap, and the next thing I knew, Butch was on the ground, holding a broken wrist. I didn't know Isabella could still move that fast.

I looked at her, shocked.

"My brothers got fired. They came home last night," she whispered to me as we were led to the office by the cafeteria monitor and part-time hippopotamus impersonator, Miss Bruntford.

Angeline and I were ready to spill the whole story, even though we knew it was going to sound like this: Isabella broke a boy's wrist because he reached for a box of cabbage juice. That was **not** going to go well for her.

While we waited for Butch's parents, we got grilled by Assistant Principal Devon.

You hate seeing a person suffer but when it's a jerk you hate it a little less.

"What happened **this** time?" he asked, looking pretty angry.

Before we could answer, Dicky piped up. "I think Butch can tell this best."

All eyes turned to the big fat and hairy oaf in the corner.

"It wasn't my fault," Butch began, and then he looked around. There were eight of us there prepared to talk. Butch knew he was heavily outnumbered.

So he confessed. Everything. Years' worth of confessions came pouring out. He said Isabella was blameless. He said it was **all his fault**.

You always wonder what makes people **mean**. Personally, I don't think anybody is born mean, because I have yet to meet a mean baby. I think that experiences have more to do with it.

Butch's dad came into the office, yelled at him, and hustled him out of the office. We watched through the window as he pushed Butch into the car, caring little about his wrist.

The next thing we knew, Isabella had run out after him.

What choice did I have? I followed. She's my best friend.

When I got there, she was leaning in the car window and talking to Butch. "Sorry about that," she said, pointing at his wrist.

He scowled at her.

"Listen, after you get patched up, why don't you join the Videogamer Club? I think you have some raw animal instincts that those punks can learn from."

Butch's face contorted from a scowl into disbelief into a genuine smile . . . and then a frown.

"This is just so you can win the membership drive, isn't it?" he said. "Like how you were trying to recruit Flartsnutt."

Isabella shook her head. "We already lost that."

Butch's dad was losing patience. "We've got to go, little girl. Back off."

Without wasting a second, Isabella grabbed the mirror on the passenger side of the car. "Hold your horses, Pops, or I'll twist this thing off," she said.

Butch's dad sputtered, and his eyes got huge. He didn't want to, but he laughed a little.

"I'll think about it," Butch told Isabella, and they drove off.

"He'll be there," Isabella said to me as we walked back inside.

I asked her why she would even want him there, and she just shrugged.

"I think it will be good."

WEDNESDAY 25

Dear Dumb Diary,

After school today, before we went to our clubs, Angeline stopped by my locker.

"Did you see the sign-up sheets? Dicky joined the Student Awareness Committee."

"What did you do, turn that charm on full blast?" I asked. "Flash those baby blues at him?"

She frowned. "That's a **rotten** thing to say, Jamie. It wasn't like that."

I knew it was a rotten thing to say, but there are very few times when you can say rotten things about baby blue eyes, and you have to make sure you don't miss them.

"You know our clubs will probably disband now," Isabella said, walking up to join us. She looked as though she didn't know what to do with her hands, so she **pulled Angeline's hair** with them a little.

"Her brothers are back," I explained, and Angeline nodded.

I decided not to tell anybody in the Cuisine Club about Dicky's decision.

Isabella told me that she wasn't going to say anything to her club, either. As we headed toward the room where the Videogamer Club met, we saw Butch going in. He **waved** at us. It was a big fat ugly hairy wave with a bandaged hand, but for Butch, it was kind of cute.

I peeked in on the Cuisine Club for just a moment, and watched the kids trying to make cookies look like turtles. Because I guess making food look like other things is a thing you want to do. **I guess.**

It was sad to think this was our last meeting.

Animals make food look like people.

Then I walked down to look in on the Student Awareness Committee meeting. I expected them to be all **celebratey**, but they weren't.

"Didn't you tell them that you won?" I asked Angeline, who stopped working on a poster for just a moment.

"I did."

"So, why aren't you all freaking out with joy and stuff?"

She raised an eyebrow at me. "Because Dicky had an idea, and we have too much work ahead of us to celebrate. I'm going to go talk to Isabella, and you need to fill in the Cuisine Club."

Can't write anymore now, Dumb D. Too tired. I'll explain tomorrow.

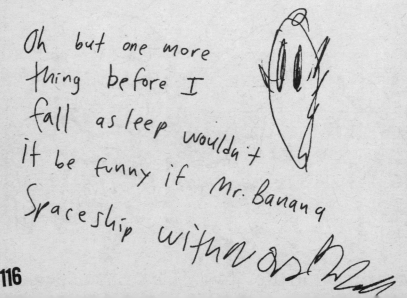

Oh but one more thing before I fall asleep wouldn't it be funny if Mr. Banana Spaceship with

Dear Dumb Diary,

Last night was a long night, but it really paid off this morning.

Dicky had an idea, all right.

He pointed out that the cafeteria was more than big enough to house all three of our clubs. Plus, the Cuisine Club was already there using the kitchen part, anyway. So why not just join all three clubs together into one big club, and split the prize three ways?

"Because, **dingledoof**," Isabella said, "that won't be enough money for anybody."

"Yes, **dingledoof**," he replied (mistaking it for a friendly nickname), "but *you* three are not going to have any problems with that. I have a plan."

MEAN NICKNAME	FRIENDLY VERSION
DINGLEDOOF	DOOFYFLOOF
DUMPYDORK	DUMPLYWUMPLY
NARGLEFART	SUZY

And so we made cupcakes. **Tons** of them. Everybody in the Cuisine Club did.

Isabella, Angeline, and Dicky came over to my house, and we were up pretty late making incredibly beautiful cupcakes. Isabella ate only three, which was awesome and kind of a miracle.

And this morning we **SOLD** the cupcakes instead of giving them away, and Angeline **sold** lemonade instead of water. And yes, she did flash the baby blues, but it was for a good cause.

Isabella and her club hauled TVs down to the lobby and hung up a sign that said **CAN YOU BEAT BUTCH?**

Everyone was eager to beat him, of course, and Isabella had a game loaded up that he wasn't familiar with. With his wrist patched up, Butch couldn't beat anyone, not even Dicky (who seemed to enjoy the games, even though they were in slight conflict with his inner personality).

Out of gratitude, I even made Dicky his very own cupcake, which he **could** eat and totally loved. (It was my fake potato cupcake recipe. It turns out that somebody besides dogs and dads actually likes cupfakes.)

Yum!

Assistant Principal Devon spontaneously approved a late start to first period just so we could carry on longer, although I suppose we should call him Uncle Dan for that.

We made more than enough money for all three clubs to keep going, and I think they'll all be better because of the overlap:

Butch will be able to interact with people without being mean to them, and Dicky will be able to interact with people without them being mean to him.

Isabella might actually look at food before she eats it, and Angeline gets to make us aware of things.

And me, I'll just get **prettier and prettier**, but this would have happened no matter what.

Oh! And the janitor that was always hanging around and staring? Turns out he really IS into cupcakes and popcorn. He's an enthusiastic amateur chef and he wanted to offer to help with the Cuisine Club, and we can really use the help now.

Since he is a janitor, I'll bet all of his recipes are spotlessly clean and free from graffiti.

FRIDAY 27

Dear Dumb Diary,

Mrs. Curie talked more about the wildebeests today, and about how living in herds protects animals. They can watch out for one another that way.

That made me think about Dicky and Butch and what makes bullies in general.

Isabella grew up the way she did because she was picked on by her mean older brothers. I'm guessing that her brothers grew up the way they did because they resented her as the baby of the family, and the fact that she was easily **ten times smarter** than they were. I mean, that **has** to wear on you. They also probably resented how pretty Isabella's best friend is.

I guess Butch might have been mean because he has it rough at home. But there's no real way for me to know that.

we're like Dicky's wildebeests

except I'm a gazelle.

I don't know if being nice to Butch will change him. He'll probably always be kind of tough, like Isabella, but I know that Dicky's problems seemed to get smaller when the truth came out about them, and that only happened when Butch saw he was outnumbered.

The wildebeests didn't even have to really attack the hyena, it was the **sheer number** of wildebeests that changed the hyena's mind.

Later on, I talked to Angeline about that, and we decided that maybe we should do some posters on that — telling people that if you're getting bullied, you should **say something**.

Isabella said that when her brothers got home, they seemed a little different. Like maybe they realized that they also were outnumbered out there in the **Terrible Real World**. It wasn't the two of them against one sister anymore — it was them against the whole world. Maybe that knocked some of the bully out of them. Maybe they'll be a little more human now, and less hyenaish.

Isabella admitted that she's glad they're back. She **hates** them, of course, but she **loves** them, of course, and she says that they keep her on edge. If she had stayed a big softy, she might not have snapped Butch's wrist like a breadstick, and somebody had to. She says the world doesn't need bullies, but as long as they're out there, it does need people that aren't afraid to stand up to them, and maybe that's kind of her deal.

Mom came home today. No phone call or anything. C'mon, Mom, even the flu season gives you a little warning.

I knew we were going to be in huge trouble, because the kitchen was a massive disaster.

At least, it was before Dad rushed in like a wildebeest and cleaned it.

Can you believe it?? **Dad actually learned how to clean**, even though I knew he never would, and Mom was less interested in the house than she was in us, anyway. I told her about some of the meals Dad hasn't been making, and he bragged to her about how great I've been taking care of him while she was gone.

Maybe I didn't know it before, but I can see now that, in our own way, we're just as Flartsnutty as any Flartsnutt you'll ever meet. Some days, maybe even a little Flartsnuttier.

Thanks for listening, Dumb Diary,

Jamie Kelly

Are You a Bully?

You could be a bully without even knowing it. Take this extremely scientific quiz to find out!

1.) There's a kid in school who brings kale salad every day for lunch. What do you say to him?
   a. "Wow, that looks . . . interesting. What is it?"
   b. "That looks like a brussels sprout ate some spinach and threw up in your lunch."
   c. Nothing. You wouldn't go near kale salad with a 10-foot pole.

2.) Your BFF proudly shows you the painting she did for art class, but it's not very good. What do you tell her?

    a. "Cool! If you want to borrow some of my glitter, I can show you some ideas for how to add a little sparkle."

    b. "Hang that in your attic to scare spiders away."

    c. "Huh. Maybe the paint spoiled."

3.) There's a kid who sits in the front of the bus every day and does math problems in a workbook for fun. What do you do?

    a. Invite him to sit with you and your friends.

    b. Steal his super-nerdy $E=mc^2$ hat and toss it around the bus until you get to school.

    c. Ignore him, just like everyone else.

4.) Your friend tries out for the soccer team, but doesn't make it. What's the first thing you say to her when she finds out?

    a. "Their loss — they'd be lucky to have you!"

    b. "I guess the coach actually wants to win some games this year, huh?"

    c. "I didn't know you played soccer."

5.) You get your Language Arts test back, and you got the highest grade in the class! What's your reaction?

a. Smile proudly and tuck the test into your folder. There's no need to brag.

b. Yell, "Take that, suckers!" and make up a special song to sing to the snotty smart kid who only got a 95%.

c. Shrug and toss it in the garbage on the way out the door. It was probably just a fluke.

6.) The girl behind you in music class has a horrible voice — and she likes to sing LOUDLY. What do you do?

a. Offer to help her learn her part. Maybe she just doesn't know the right notes!

b. Say, "Hey thanks, I always wondered what six cats and a dozen golf balls would sound like in the dryer."

c. Wear earplugs. Not your problem!

7.) You accidentally splash your elderly neighbor when you ride your bike through a puddle. How do you handle it?

a. Apologize profusely, and offer to do her laundry for free.

b. Laugh and holler, "10 points!" before pedaling furiously away.

c. Keep riding without looking back.

If you answered . . .

Mostly As: You're a perfectly polite specimen, without a bullying bone in your body. Either that, or you hide it well. Either way, bully for you!

Mostly Bs: Hate to break it to you, pal, but you're the kind of a bully with a capital B. You might want to scale it back a bit, or the nerds and dweebs of the world might decide to gang up on you one day.

Mostly Cs: You don't try to be a bully, but you don't try NOT to, either. And that's almost just as bad. Maybe just try something, sometime, ever, instead of ignoring everything.

DEAR DUMB DIARY

CAN'T GET ENOUGH OF JAMIE KELLY?
CHECK OUT HER OTHER DEAR DUMB DIARY BOOKS!

YEAR TWO: #1: School. Hasn't This
Gone On Long Enough?

YEAR TWO: #2: The Super-Nice
are Super-Annoying

YEAR TWO: #3: Nobody's Perfect.
I'm As Close As It Gets.

YEAR TWO: #4: What I Don't
Know Might Hurt Me

#1: Let's Pretend This
Never Happened

#2: My Pants Are
Haunted!

#3: Am I the Princess or
the Frog?

#4: Never Do
Anything, Ever

5: Can Adults Become
Human?

#6: The Problem With Here
Is That It's Where I'm From

#7: Never Underestimate
Your Dumbness

#8: It's Not My Fault I
Know Everything

9: That's What Friends
<u>Aren't</u> For

#10: The Worst Things In
Life Are Also Free

#11: Okay, So Maybe I Do
Have Superpowers

#12: Me! (Just Like You,
Only Better)

Our Dumb Diary:
A Journal to Share

Totally Not Boring
School Planner

candy APPLE

Read them all!

Life, Starring Me!

Callie for Preside[nt]

Drama Queen

I've Got a Secret

Confessions of a Bitter
Secret Santa

Super Sweet 13

The Boy Next Door

The Sister Switch

Snowfall Surprise

Rumor Has It

The Sweetheart Deal

The Accidental
Cheerleader

The Babysitting Wars

Star-Crossed

Accidentally
Fabulous

Accidentally
Famous

Accidentally
Fooled

Accidentally
Friends

w to Be a Girly Girl in
Just Ten Days

Ice Dreams

Juicy Gossip

Making Waves

Miss Popularity

Miss Popularity
Goes Camping

Miss Popularity
and the Best Friend Disaster

Totally Crushed

ish You Were Here,
Liza

See You Soon,
Samantha

Miss You, Mina

Winner Takes All

POISON APPLE BOOKS

The Dead End

This Totally Bites!

Miss Fortune

Now You See Me...

Midnight Howl

Her Evil Twin

Curiosity Killed the Cat

At First Bite

**THRILLING.
BONE-CHILLIN
THESE BOOK
HAVE BITE!**

Danny Shine just wants to draw comics.
But first, he has to get his name off of

THE LOSER LIST

Read them all!

About Jim Benton

Jim Benton is not a middle-school girl, but do not hold that against him. He has managed to make a living out of being funny, anyway.

He is the creator of many licensed properties, some for big kids, some for little kids, and some for grown-ups who, frankly, are probably behaving like little kids.

You may already know his properties: It's Happy Bunny™ or Catwad™, and of course you already know about Dear Dumb Diary.

He's created a kids' TV series, designed clothing, and written books.

Jim Benton lives in Michigan with his spectacular wife and kids. They do not have a dog, and they especially do not have a vengeful beagle. This is his first series for Scholastic.

Jamie Kelly has no idea that Jim Benton, or you, or anybody is reading her diaries. So, please, please, please don't tell her.